FOODS FROM
ITALY
GOLRIZ GOLKAR
childsworld.com

Published by The Child's World®
800-599-READ · www.childsworld.com

Photography Credits
Photographs ©: iStockphoto, cover (background), 1 (background), 3 (background), 12; Shutterstock Images, cover (flag), 1 (flag), 3 (flag), 4 (flag), 5 (globe), 16–17; Boyko Pictures/Shutterstock Images, 4 (landmarks), back cover; Peter Hermes Furian/Shutterstock Images, 5 (country); Odua Images/Shutterstock Images, 6–7; Francesco Vignali/iStockphoto, 9; Alvaro German Vilela/Shutterstock Images, 11; Marco Mayer/Shutterstock Images, 14–15; Sergii Kumer/Shutterstock Images, 18; Alena Kos/Shutterstock Images, 20; Tanya Sid/Shutterstock Images, 22

ISBN Information
9781503885325 (Reinforced Library Binding)
9781503885677 (Portable Document Format)
9781503886315 (Online Multi-user eBook)
9781503886957 (Electronic Publication)

LCCN 2023937427

Printed in the United States of America

Golriz Golkar is a former elementary school teacher. She has written more than 70 books for children. She enjoys reading, looking for ladybugs, and baking with her young daughter.

TABLE OF CONTENTS

ITALY

Italy is a country in southern Europe. Its northern border touches France, Switzerland, Austria, and Slovenia. The rest of the country is surrounded by water. Italy has two main islands, Sicily and Sardinia. They lie in the Mediterranean Sea. Italian summers are hot and dry. Winters are cool and wet. Mountainous areas can be snowy. Coastal areas have warmer temperatures. Italy is famous for many delicious foods that are enjoyed around the world.

Italian **cuisine** varies by **region**. Northern dishes have lots of dairy. Olive oil and tomatoes are common in the south. Meat dishes are popular in central Italy.

Italians in coastal and island regions eat more fish. Some foods such as pizza and pasta are eaten all over the country.

Many Italians love food. They sometimes take long lunch breaks. They enjoy big feasts with special foods on holidays and other important occasions. Even the Italian government takes food seriously. It makes sure that regional foods are labeled as **authentic**. This helps people know they are eating the real thing!

CHAPTER 1

PIZZA MARGHERITA

Pizza is a famous Italian food. It was first made in the southern Italian city of Naples. Pizza in southern Italy has a thin crust. The crust is thicker in the north.

There are many flavors of pizza. One of the most popular is *pizza margherita.* Legend says it is named after an Italian queen. In 1889, Queen Margherita of Italy visited Naples. She noticed the smell of pizza. A man named Raffaele Esposito was making it in his **pizzeria**. He claimed the queen invited him to the royal palace to make different kinds of pizza.

Families can enjoy making pizza together.

The queen picked her favorite one. Esposito named it “pizza margherita.” Similar recipes had been published earlier. And experts today doubt this story is true. But Esposito made the margherita pizza famous.

Pizza margherita is a thin-crust pizza made with few ingredients. It is red, white, and green. These are the colors of the Italian flag. To make the pizza, dough is rolled by hand into a large circle. Then it is covered with tomato sauce. This sauce is often made with San Marzano tomatoes. These tomatoes have a sweet, rich flavor.

Wood-fired pizza ovens can cook a pizza in just a few minutes.

Slices of milky, fresh mozzarella cheese are arranged on the dough. Basil leaves go on top of the cheese. Olive oil is drizzled all over. The pizza is baked in a wood-fired oven. When it is done, it has melty cheese and a crispy crust. Its sweet and salty flavors make this dish a favorite.

TAGLIATELLE ALLA BOLOGNESE

Pasta is another favorite Italian dish. There are many different pasta shapes. Pasta can be made with different ingredients and sauces. One famous dish is *tagliatelle alla Bolognese* (tahl-yah-TEL-lay AL-lah boh-loh-NYAY-zay). Tagliatelle is pasta made from fresh eggs and cut into long ribbons. It comes from northern Italy. Tagliatelle is often served with a tomato-and-meat sauce called *ragù* (ra-GOO) *alla Bolognese.* This is known in English as Bolognese sauce.

Pasta-making machines help cooks roll and cut their pasta so it is all the same size. Pasta can also be rolled and cut by hand.

TASTY TAGLIATELLE

Tagliatelle was first made in Bologna, Italy. The city hall printed an official recipe that is kept in its files. A golden sculpture of a tagliatella noodle is stored in the city hall, too. It shows the exact measurements a noodle should be.

Bolognese sauce must cook for several hours.

To make tagliatelle, pasta dough is rolled out into a large circle. It is folded over itself many times. Then it is cut into long ribbons. Sometimes tagliatelle dough includes spinach. This makes the pasta green.

Traditional Bolognese sauce takes a while to cook. Chopped Italian bacon called *pancetta* (pan-CHET-tah) is fried in a pan. Celery, carrots, onions, and garlic are added. Ground beef, **veal**, or pork is mixed in. A runny tomato sauce called *passata* (pah-SAH-tah) is added. Some recipes include milk or broth. The sauce cooks for about three hours.

Tagliatelle alla Bolognese is a favorite Italian dish.

When the ragù is almost ready, the tagliatelle is cooked. It goes in boiling water for a few minutes. Then it is drained. The sauce and the pasta are mixed together. Parmesan cheese makes a perfect topping. The silky pasta perfectly holds the sweet sauce. The cheese gives a little salty taste. It is a **hearty** meal.

CHAPTER 3

TIRAMISÙ

Italy has many famous desserts. One of the most popular is *tiramisù* (teer-ah-mee-SOO). This dessert comes from northeastern Italy. But two different regions claim to be the home of tiramisù. Some people think it was first made in Veneto in the 1900s. Others say the dessert came from Friuli-Venezia Giulia. They say it is older than the 1900s. In 2017, the Italian government decided that tiramisù came from Friuli. March 21 became World Tiramisù Day. Every year, people celebrate the arrival of spring with this dessert!

Tiramisù is a classic Italian dessert with many variations.

DIFFERENT KINDS OF TIRAMISÙ

Veneto and Friuli both claim tiramisù as a regional dessert. However, Friuli is home to different versions of the recipe. The earliest known recipe uses cake and Marsala wine instead of ladyfingers and espresso. There is no mascarpone cheese in the creamy layers. Another version uses a light semi-frozen cream called *semifreddo* (seh-mee-FREHD-doh). The traditional version with ladyfingers and espresso was first published in 1981. This recipe was from Veneto.

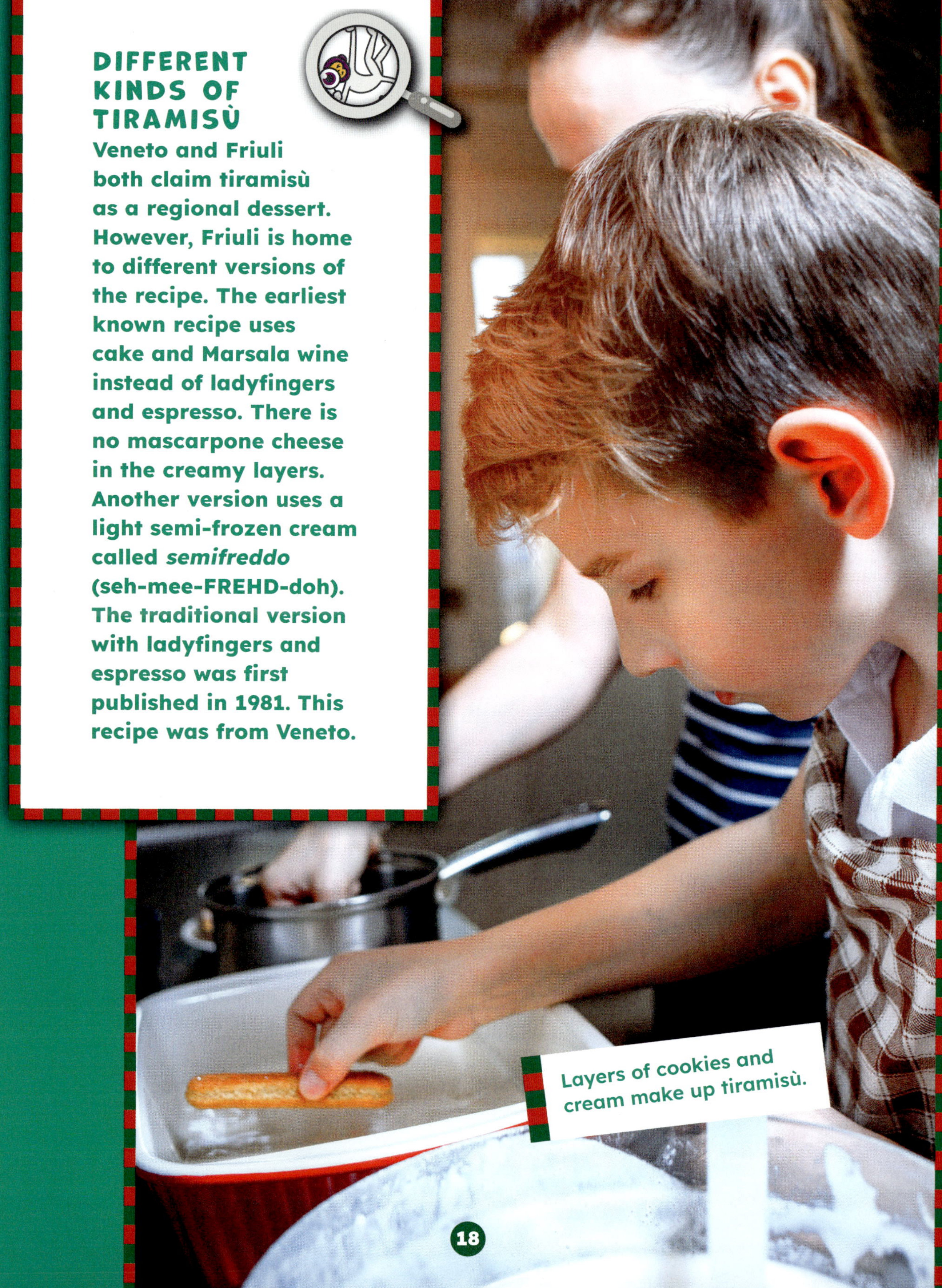

Layers of cookies and cream make up tiramisù.

Tiramisù is usually made with biscuit cookies called *savoiardi* (sah-voy-YAR-dee). These are also called ladyfingers. They are dipped in espresso, a strong coffee. Some recipes use Marsala wine instead of coffee. The dessert also has a cream filling. It is made with mascarpone cheese, cream, sugar, and vanilla mixed together. Some recipes also include eggs.

The dipped biscuits are placed side by side in a serving dish. They form a layer. Then a cream layer is spread on top of the biscuit layer. Another layer of dipped biscuits comes next. The dessert is finished with a final layer of cream. Then cocoa powder or chocolate shavings are sprinkled across the top.

Tiramisù can be cut like a cake or served individually.

After that, the dessert is ready to be sliced and served. Sometimes, tiramisù is prepared in individual cups instead. No matter how it is made, it is always sweet and creamy.

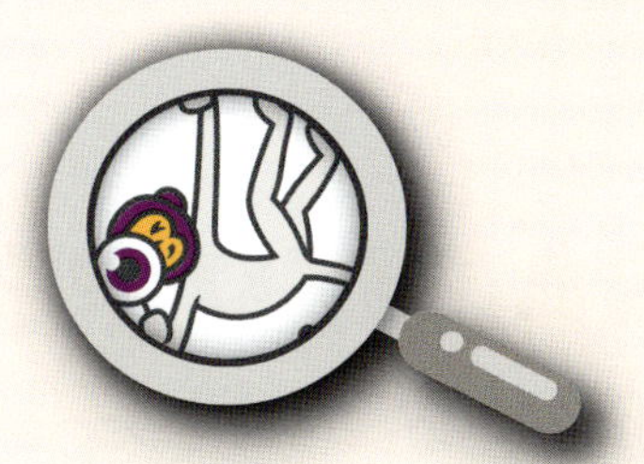

WONDER MORE

Wondering about New Information

How much did you know about the history of pizza before reading this book? What new information did you learn? Write down three new facts you learned from this book. Was the new information surprising? Why or why not?

Wondering How It Matters

Why do you think it is important to learn about foods from different countries? How can learning about and trying new foods affect your life? Are there any foods from Italy you would like to try?

Wondering Why

Italians often like to follow authentic recipes, and every Italian region is proud of its own recipes. Why do you think it is important for these regions to follow their authentic recipes? How is this important for Italian people and the world?

Ways to Keep Wondering

Learning about foods from other countries can be a complex topic. After reading this book, what questions do you have about foods from Italy? What can you do to learn more about the history of these foods?

TIRAMISÙ RECIPE

With an adult's help, make this easy and family-friendly tiramisù recipe. It has no caffeine, alcohol, or raw eggs.

Ingredients

- 1 ½ cups heavy whipping cream
- 8 ounces mascarpone cheese
- ⅓ cup sugar
- 1 teaspoon vanilla
- 1 ½ cups cold decaffeinated espresso
- 1 box (about 30) ladyfingers
- Cocoa powder for dusting
- Fresh raspberries or strawberries (optional)

Steps

1. Whip the heavy cream in a large mixing bowl. Use an electric mixer if possible. Slowly add the sugar and vanilla to the bowl. Keep mixing until the cream forms stiff peaks when the mixer is removed. Add the mascarpone cheese and mix until all ingredients are combined.

2. With an adult's help, prepare the espresso. Pour it into a small bowl and let it cool. Dip ladyfingers one by one into the espresso. Do not oversoak them. Lay them side by side in a pan or serving dish about 8 by 8 inches in size. Spread about half of the cream filling over this biscuit layer.

3. Dip the remaining ladyfingers in the espresso and make another layer in the dish. Spread the remaining cream filling over the new biscuit layer to finish the dessert.

4. Dust the top of the tiramisù with cocoa powder. Top with fresh raspberries or strawberries if desired. Refrigerate for at least three hours before serving.

GLOSSARY

authentic (aw-THEHN-tik) Something authentic is made or done the same way as the original. Many Italians use authentic ingredients when cooking dishes.

cuisine (kwih-ZEEN) A cuisine is a style of cooking. Italian cuisine is enjoyed all over the world.

hearty (HAR-tee) Something that is hearty is filling and rich. A hearty meal can keep a person full for hours.

pizzeria (peet-zuh-REE-yuh) A pizzeria is a place where pizza is made and sold. A pizzeria can sell many kinds of pizza.

region (REE-jun) A region is a geographic or cultural area. Italian food is different depending on the region it comes from.

traditional (truh-DIH-shuh-nul) Something traditional is handed down from age to age and follows past practices. Traditional Italian recipes often have specific ingredients that do not change over time.

veal (VEEL) Veal is the meat from a young cow. Veal is often used in tagliatelle alla Bolognese.

FIND OUT MORE

In the Library

Doeden, Matt. *Travel to Italy.* Minneapolis, MN: Lerner, 2023.

Mattern, Joanne. *Pizza.* Minneapolis, MN: Bellwether Media, 2020.

Perkins, Chloe. *Italy.* New York, NY: Simon Spotlight, 2016.

On the Web

Visit our website for links about foods from Italy:
childsworld.com/links

Note to Parents, Caregivers, Teachers, and Librarians: We routinely verify our Web links to make sure they are safe and active sites. So encourage your readers to check them out!

INDEX